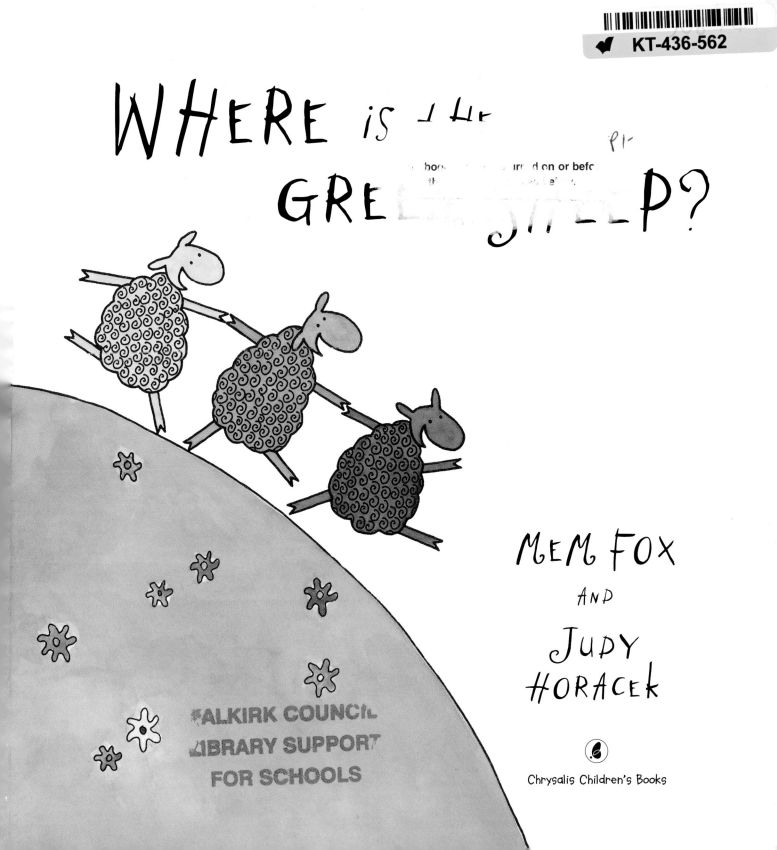

WHERE IS THE GREEN SHEEP?

MEM FOX
AND
JUDY HORACEK

Chrysalis Children's Books

First published by Penguin Books Australia,
a division of Pearson Australia Group Pty Ltd, 2004
First published in Great Britain in 2005 by Chrysalis Children's Books,
an imprint of Chrysalis Books Group Plc
The Chrysalis Building, Bramley Road, London W10 6SP
www.chrysalisbooks.co.uk

A CIP catalogue record for this book is available from the British Library.

ISBN 1 84458 367 8

Text and cover design by Deborah Brash © Penguin Group (Australia)
Typeset in 27/40pt Gazette
Colour reproduction by Splitting Image, Clayton, Victoria
Printed and bound by Imago Productions, Singapore

2 4 6 8 10 9 7 5 3 1

This book can be ordered direct from the publisher. Please contact
the Marketing Department. But try your bookshop first.

Here is the blue sheep.

And here is the red sheep.

Here is the bath sheep.

And here is the bed sheep.

But where is the green sheep?

Here is the thin sheep,
and here is the wide sheep.

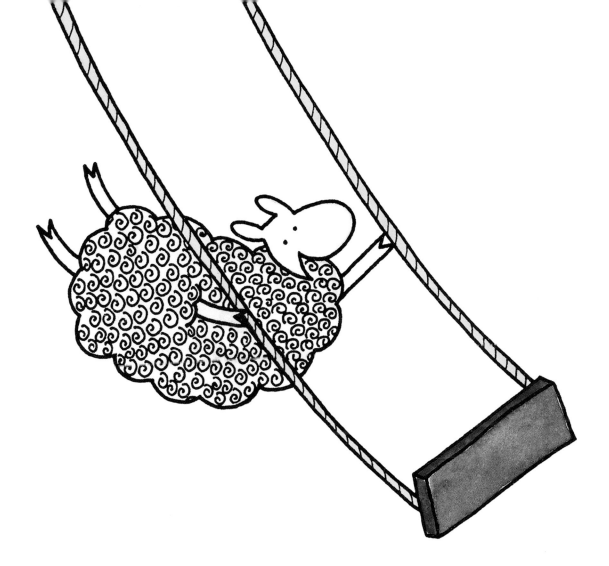

Here is the swing sheep.

And here is the slide sheep.

But where is the green sheep?

Here is the up sheep,

and here is the down sheep.

Here is the band sheep.

And here is the clown sheep.

But where is the green sheep?

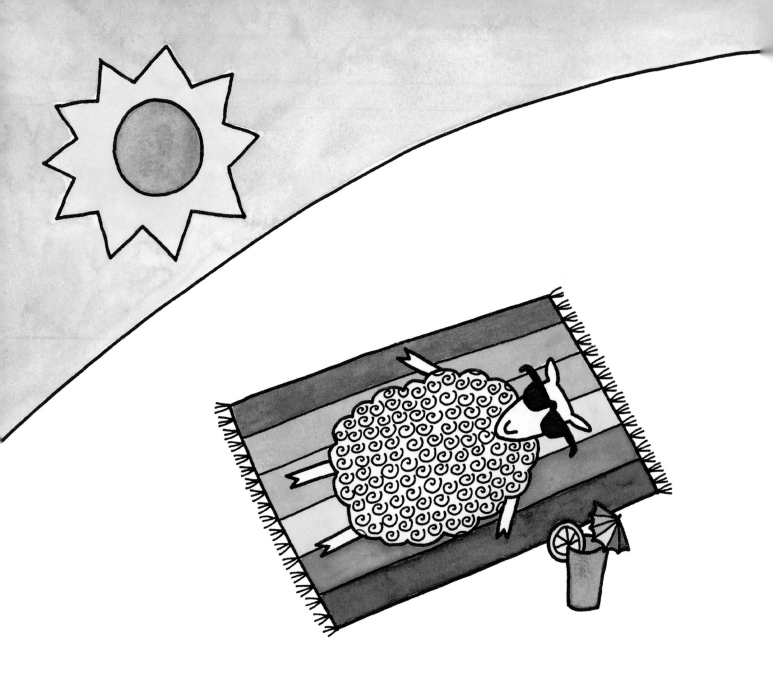

Here is the sun sheep.

And here is the rain sheep.

Here is the car sheep,
and here is the train sheep.

But where is the green sheep?

Here is the wind sheep.

And here is the wave sheep.

Here is the scared sheep,
and here is the brave sheep.

But where is the green sheep?

Here is the near sheep.

And here is the far sheep.

Here is the moon sheep.

And here is the star sheep.

But where is the green sheep?

Where IS that green sheep?